CLASSIC FAIRY TALES

The UGLY Duckling

Retold by Sally Grindley

Illustrated by Bert Kitchen

MACDONALD YOUNG BOOKS

First published in Great Britain in 1996
by Macdonald Young Books
61 Western Road
Hove
East Sussex BN3 1JD

Designed by Shireen Nathoo Design

Typeset in 20pt Minion
Printed and bound in Belgium by Proost International Book Co.

British Library Cataloguing in Publication Data available.

ISBN: 0 7500 1998 0
ISBN: 0 7500 1999 9 (pb)

Once upon a time, a mother duck sat on her nest amongst the tall reeds by the side of a river. All around her, the summer sun was ripening wheat in the fields and on the river, families of ducks were already bobbing up and down. She wondered how much longer she would have to sit there alone waiting for her eggs to hatch.

At last, the eggs began to crack: first one, then another, then two, then another, then one more. "Peep peep!" cried the ducklings as they stuck their heads out of their shells and looked around.

"Quack quack!" Their mother greeted them proudly and stood to look at her brood. But then she saw that one egg still lay in the nest, big and round and unbroken.

"Goodness gracious, how much longer must I wait for this egg to hatch?"

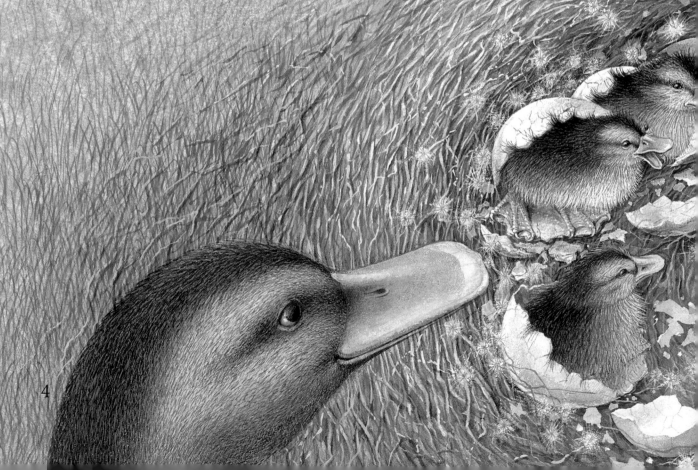

"Are you sure it's not a turkey egg?" said an old duck who happened to be waddling past. "It's certainly big enough. Take my advice and leave it there. You'll have no end of trouble teaching a turkey how to swim."

The old duck waddled on, but the mother duck went back to sitting on the egg while her young ones toddled around beside her.

At last, the big egg cracked. There was a loud "peep peep" and the youngest duckling tumbled out. He was very big, and he wasn't at all like his brothers and sisters. His mother looked at him and wondered for a moment if the old duck had been right. Well, she was going to make him swim and prove her wrong.

The next day, she took her ducklings down to the river's edge. One by one they plunged into the water after her, bobbed to the surface and floated happily along, even the big duckling.

"Well, he can swim," said the mother duck, watching her youngest son swimming beautifully, "even if he is a bit odd-looking."

After their swim, she took her brood to the farmyard to introduce them to all the other birds who lived there. It was a noisy place, crowded with families of ducks and hens, many of them squabbling about who was best at this and who was worst at that.

"Quack! Quack!" said the mother duck, walking proudly along with her head held high. "Now keep in line, waddle don't walk,

turn out your toes, quack 'good morning' to the other ducks," she ordered her ducklings. "Nod your heads to the old duck over there. She is the most important fowl in these parts."

Other ducks clamoured to watch the new arrivals. "Here, look at this lot!" they said. And, "Look at that big, ugly one at the back!"

With that, one of the ducks ran over and bit the big duckling on the neck. "Go away," he said. "We don't want you here."

"Leave him alone," said the mother duck. "He's not doing you any harm."

"He's big, and he's ugly, and he doesn't look like everyone else," replied the duck. "He deserves to be bitten."

The important old duck waddled over and complimented the mother on her brood. "A good-looking bunch, all except that one," she remarked, pointing to the big duckling. "He's quite the ugliest youngster I've ever seen."

"He may not be handsome, but he is very good-natured and he swims well. I'm sure his looks will improve as he gets older. He was in his egg too long, that's all."

They made themselves at home, but the big duckling was pushed and shoved and bitten and laughed at all day and every day. The hens snapped, "You're too big!" The ducks snapped, "You're too clumsy!" The turkey cock snapped, "We don't want you!" Even his brothers and sisters snapped, "We hope the cat gets you, you ugly great thing."

The poor duckling had no friends and grew more and more unhappy. "How I wish I wasn't so ugly," he said to himself over and over again. When even his mother, in a moment of despair, said, "Perhaps it would have been better if you hadn't been born," he could bear it no longer.

The ugly duckling ran away. He ran and ran until he came to a great stretch of marshland. Too tired and miserable to go any further, he lay his head on his wings and fell into an unhappy sleep.

In the morning he was woken by a family
of wild ducks, who said that he could stay
but only if he kept right away from them.
Wild geese lived there as well, and the ugly
duckling cheered up when two young ones
were friendly to him. But two days later shots
rang out and the young geese fell down dead
among the reeds.

Now there was gunfire everywhere. Blue smoke billowed around, and the shouts of hunters cut across the hysterical squawking and flapping of wings as wild geese and ducks tried to escape. Hound dogs came splashing through the mud, crashing through the reeds, barking and howling.

The poor duckling was terrified. He stood quivering among the reeds and was about to

14

tuck his head under his wing to hide, when a dog's face appeared inches from him. Its red tongue was hanging out and it snarled and bared its sharp white teeth – but then suddenly it ran off without even touching him.

"Thank goodness!" sighed the duckling. "I am so ugly even the dog has run away from me."

He cowered where he was until at last the shooting stopped. Even then he could not move, he was so frightened. Hours passed before he ran from the marshes, across the fields and meadows, struggling against the stormy wind. As night fell, he came upon a tumbledown farmhouse, where he found a gap in the door and squeezed his way in.

An old woman lived there with her cat and her hen. They found the duckling in the morning and allowed him to stay provided he lay eggs for them. Being a drake, he couldn't, of course, and the cat and the hen made fun of him. He grew tired of their cruel teasing and began to miss the fresh air and sunshine. After a while, he felt a tremendous urge to go swimming and feel the sun on his feathers. And so he went on his way again.

He found a lake where he could float and
dive and bob about. But winter quickly came,
and biting winds and hail and snow chilled
the duckling to the bone. As he sat shivering
one day, watching the sun set, he saw a flock
of beautiful birds fly out from the rushes and
circle higher and higher in the sky. Their
feathers glistened white as the unspoilt snow
on the ground and their necks stretched long
and graceful. They spread their powerful
wings and gave a loud cry, which the ugly

duckling couldn't help but return with his
own piercing screech. He stretched his neck
towards the sky as if trying to reach out to
them, and watched the beautiful birds until
they were just dots on the horizon. Deep
down inside he felt a strange longing, which
lasted many days after they had gone and
turned into great unhappiness. He had never
seen such birds before, yet he yearned to be
with them.

Now winter bit harder and harder. The lake began to freeze and the little duckling swam round and round to keep a hole for himself. He paddled his feet frantically, but at last he was too exhausted to move. He sat as if in a dream and soon he was frozen tight.

As luck would have it, a farmer passed by early next morning and saw him. He broke the ice and lifted the duckling free. He carefully tucked him inside his coat and took him home to his wife, who nursed him back to life. But the farmer's children were noisy

and boisterous, and when they tried to play
with the duckling they frightened him. In
panic he blundered into a milk pail then flew
into a big bowl of butter and then into a
barrel of flour. The farmer's wife chased him
and the children laughed and screamed as

they fell on top of one another trying to catch him. The duckling was petrified, but he managed to scramble out through an open door and hide under some bushes in the freshly fallen snow. There he lay for hours, cold, unhappy and unloved.

The winter months continued long and hard. The duckling wandered from place to place, not knowing where he was going and wishing at times that he had stayed at the farmyard.

And then at last spring arrived. The duckling was lying among the reeds in the marshes when the warmth from the sun and the song of the larks woke him. He stood and stretched out his wings and was surprised to feel how strong and powerful they had become.

He moved into the open and took off into the air. Up and up he flew into the clear blue sky. Soon he had left the marshes far behind and was flying over a beautiful garden full of apple blossom. Alongside ran a winding

stream, where lilac bushes spread their branches over the water. From beneath them came three swans, floating majestically and preening their feathers.

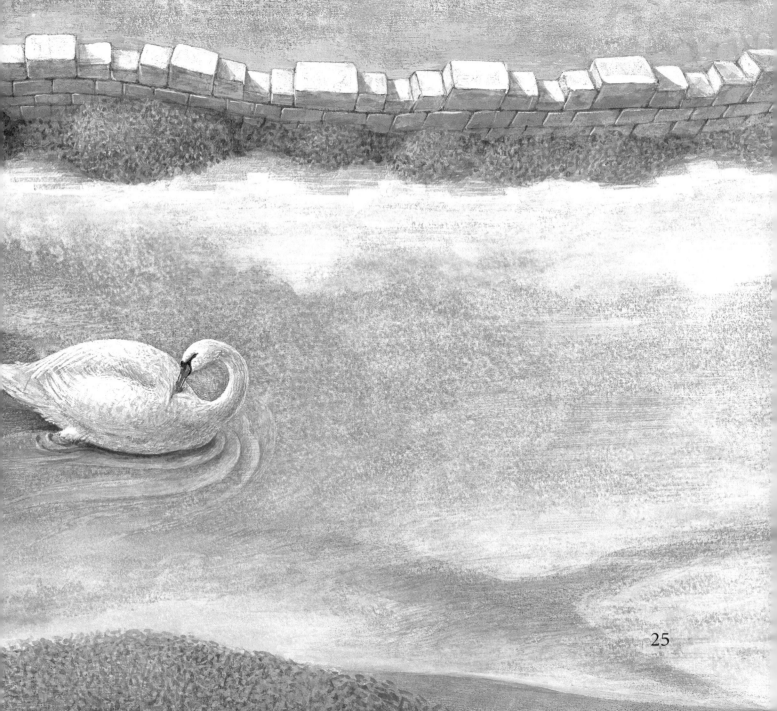

As soon as he saw the birds, the ugly duckling once again felt the deep sense of longing that he had felt so many months before.

"I shall fly over to them and greet them!" he said. "Yet how dare I, the ugliest bird who ever lived, go near such wonderful, noble birds? They'll probably attack me, but better

to be killed by them than to be bitten by ducks and pecked by hens and chased by people; or to suffer such a winter again."

He flew down and landed on the water and nervously swam towards the beautiful swans. When they saw him they swam in his direction.

"They're coming to kill me," whispered the ugly duckling. He bent his head down meekly in readiness. But as he did he saw something in the clear, sparkling water. It was his own reflection, yet he was no longer grey. His feathers glistened white in the sunshine. His neck was long and graceful, and when he unfolded his wings he saw at last that he was no longer an ugly duckling. He was a swan! He was a beautiful swan!

Now he could hold his head up high.
When he did he found that the other swans
had made a circle around him. They didn't

chase him away. Instead, they caressed him gently with their beaks, and for the first time in his life he knew what it was like to love and be loved.

Other titles available in the Classic Fairy Tales series: